The Wonderful Wizard of Oz

L. Frank Baum

ABOUT YOUR BOOK

MP3	Go to Helbling e-zone to listen to or download the activity
(headphones icon)	Listen to the story
(speech bubbles icon)	Talk about the story
glossary•	When you see the red dot, check the word in the glossary
K	Prepare for Cambridge English Exams: Key
FACT FILE	Read informative fact files which develop themes from the story
e-zone	Go to Helbling e-zone to do activities

FOR THE TEACHER

A state-of-the-art interactive learning environment with 1000s of free online self-correcting activities for your chosen readers.

Go to our Readers Resource site for information on using readers and downloadable Resource Sheets, photocopiable Worksheets and Answer Keys. Plus free sample tracks from the story.
www.helblingreaders.com

For lots of great ideas on using Graded Readers consult Reading Matters, the Teacher's Guide to using Helbling Readers.

Contents

HELBLING DIGITAL

INTERACTIVE ONLINE TEACHING AND LEARNING MATERIALS

e·zone
THE EDUCATIONAL PLATFORM

HELBLING e-zone is an inspiring new state-of-the-art, easy-to-use interactive learning environment.

Use the **personal access code** on the inside back cover of this book to unlock a host of self-correcting activities, including:

- reading comprehension;
- listening comprehension;
- vocabulary;
- grammar;
- exam preparation.

TEACHERS register free of charge to set up classes and assign individual and class homework sets. Results are provided automatically once the deadline has been reached and detailed reports on performance are available at a click.

STUDENTS test their language skills in a stimulating interactive environment. All activities can be attempted as many times as necessary and full results and feedback are given as soon as the deadline has been reached. Single student access is also available.

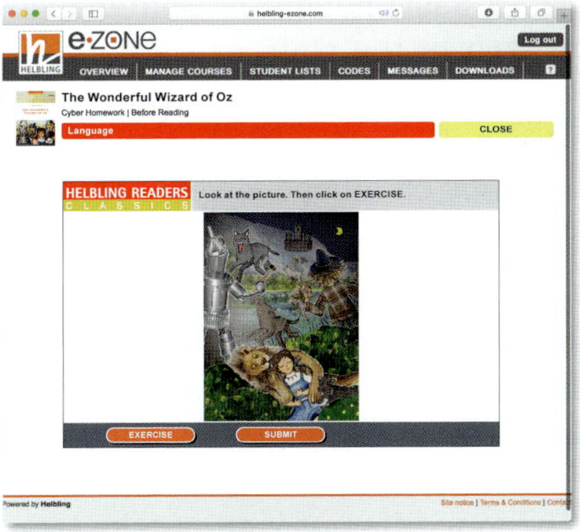

1000s of free online interactive activities now available for HELBLING READERS and your other favourite Helbling Languages publications.

ONLINE ACTIVITIES

helbling-ezone.com

blog.helblingreaders.com

Love reading and readers and can't wait to get your class interested? Have a class library and reading programme but not sure how to take it a step further? The Helbling Readers BLOG is the place for you.

The **Helbling Readers BLOG** will provide you with ideas on setting up and running a Book Club and tips on reading lessons **every week**.

- Book Club
- Worksheets
- Lesson Plans

Subscribe to our **BLOG** and you will never miss out on our updates.

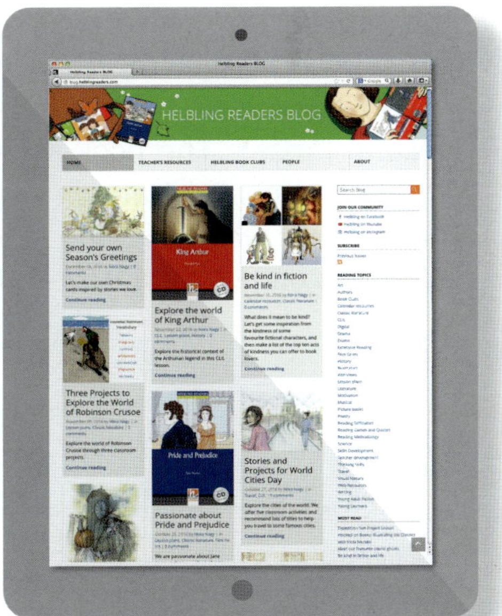

ABOUT THE AUTHOR

Lynam Frank Baum is born in Chittenango, a small town in the state of New York in 1856. His father is a businessman and the family is rich. Frank has eight brothers and sisters and his childhood is very happy.

He is a shy•, quiet boy and his health• isn't very good. He doesn't go to school and he studies at home with a teacher. He loves reading. His favourite stories are traditional European fairy tales but he doesn't like the violence and the frightening creatures• in them. When he writes *The Wonderful Wizard of Oz* at the age of 44, he wants to write a different kind of fairy tale.
Baum has many jobs before he becomes a successful writer. He is a journalist, a chicken farmer, a salesman• and an actor. He manages his own theatre and writes plays for it. He even has a shop. But most of his careers end in failure•. In 1882 Baum marries Maud Gage. Together they have four sons.
In 1897 he writes a book of nursery rhymes in story form: Mother Goose in Prose•. The book sells well and Baum decides to stop working and concentrate on writing. In 1900 he publishes *The Wonderful Wizard of Oz* and it is an immediate success.
Baum dies on 6 May, 1919 and is buried in California.

GLOSSARY

- **creatures:** animals, etc
- **failure:** the opposite of success
- **health:** how he feels
- **prose:** ordinary written language, in contrast to poetry
- **salesman:** man who sells things
- **shy:** quiet and not sure of himself

ABOUT THE BOOK

The Wonderful Wizard of Oz is the story of a little girl called Dorothy. It describes her adventures when she and her dog are carried away during a cyclone• to the magical land of Oz. There she meets a kind witch who tells her to go to the Emerald• City and ask the Wizard to help her go back home. Dorothy follows the yellow brick road to the Emerald City and on her way she makes three friends: the Scarecrow, the Tin Woodman and the Cowardly• Lion. When they get to the Emerald City the Wizard tells them that first they must kill the Wicked Witch of the West. So the four friends set off once more for the land of the Winkies where the terrible witch lives.

The Wonderful Wizard of Oz is a modern fairy tale. Baum mixes reality (scarecrows and cornfields) with the fantasy and magic of traditional European fairy tales (wizards and witches). Dorothy lives on the dry, grey prairies• of Kansas. Her life is boring and her dog Toto is her only friend. Oz is full of colour. There are castles, talking animals, witches and dark forests. She makes new friends and has many exciting adventures. But in the end Dorothy learns that there's no place like home!

The book is translated into over 50 languages and millions of children and adults know and love the story.

Do you know?

The name Oz comes from Baum's filing cabinet• for documents from O-Z.

- **cowardly:** without courage; not brave
- **cyclone:** strong wind
- **emerald:** precious green stone
- **filing cabinet:** cupboard with many drawers where you put documents and letters
- **prairies:** large areas of flat grassy land in North America

NEW FACT FILE

ALL ABOUT Alliteration

The name **'Wicked Witch of the West'** has three words next to each other that begin with the same sound. They all begin with the letter **W**. This is a clear example of how fairy tales make use of that powerful poetic device• called **alliteration**.

alliteration (n.) the repetition of the same sounds at the beginning of words.
'Henry hurries home to do his homework', or 'A rabbit running over roses' are simple examples of how alliteration can be used in a sentence. It is important to remember, however, that it is the sound, and not the letter of the alphabet that must be the same. For example, the 's' in 'shy' does not alliterate with the 's' in sun, because they do not have the same sound.

SAY IT!

Which of these words alliterates with **sun**? Say them aloud first!

- **sure**
- **summer**
- **circle**
- **swim**

GLOSSARY

- **alliterative:** that use alliteration
- **poetic device:** tool a poet uses to add meaning, rhythm, etc.

Alliteration is used in all types of literature, but mostly in poetry. Many of our favourite characters have alliterative names: Bugs Bunny, Donald Duck, King Kong, Mickey Mouse, Woody Woodpecker. And in the language that we use every day there are lots of common phrases that use alliteration:

BACK TO BASICS

JUMP FOR JOY

GREEN AS GRASS

And in many tongue twisters, too, words that begin with the same sound are placed close together:

'A busy buzzing bumblebee went busily buzzing by'

'She sells sea shells by the seashore'

Over to you

Can you find other examples of alliteration in everyday language?

Do you know other fantasy characters with alliterative names?

Write a sentence using alliteration of the sound of your first name (Eg. 'Michael makes money'). Then do the same with the names of your classmates.

SAY IT!

How quickly can you say them? Time yourself and a friend.

The Wizard of Oz

Aunt Em
Glinda
The Wicked Witch of the West
Uncle Henry

BEFORE READING

1 ▶ MP3 **Listen to Dorothy talking about herself and her home. Complete the text with the words in the box.**

cyclones	dog	grass	orphan	prairie	stove

A I haven't got a mother and father. I'm an .... I live with my Aunt Em and Uncle Henry in Kansas.

B I live on a farm on the .... The land is flat and covered with ....

C My best friend is my .... Toto. I love him very much.

D There are often .... in Kansas. They are very strong winds.

E My house has one room. There's a .... for cooking, a cupboard, a table, some chairs and our beds.

2 **Look at the pictures of three characters Dorothy meets in the Land of Oz. Match the words below to the numbers.**

The Scarecrow

The Tin Woodman

The Cowardly Lion

a ☐ axe **b** ☐ paws **c** ☐ pole **d** ☐ straw

3 **Now use the words in the sentences below.**

a .... is made from the dry stems of corn.
b A .... is a long piece of wood or metal.
c An .... is a tool for cutting down trees.
d The .... of animals like cats, dogs and bears are their feet.

4 **Complete the sentences with the correct adjective.**

brave clever kind

a If you have courage you are ....
b If you have a heart you are ....
c If you have a brain you are ....

5 **The three characters in Exercise 2 want to have courage, a brain and a heart. Who wants what? Share your ideas with a partner.**

BEFORE READING

1 Write the names of the animals under the photos.

bee   crow   monkey   mouse   stork   wolf

a ....

b ....

c ....

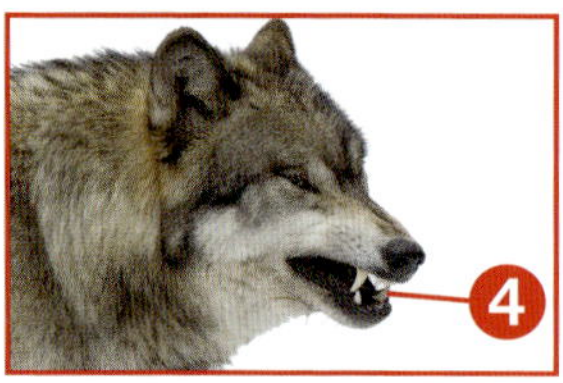

d ....

e ....

f ....

2 Look again at the photos in Exercise 1. Match the numbered parts with the words below.

a ☐ arm   **b** ☐ beak   **c** ☐ tail
d ☐ sting   **e** ☐ teeth   **f** ☐ wing

3 K Use the letters below to complete the verbs.

C E E F I N S T Y

a What can animals do with their teeth? B _ T _
b What can birds and insects do with their wings? _ L _
c What can birds do with their beaks? P _ _ K
d What can bees do with their stings? _ _ I _ G

4 **Write the names of the cardinal points on the compass.**

north south east west

a ....

b ....

c ....

d ....

5 **MP3** **Listen and match the names of three of the lands in Oz with where they are.**

a ☐ The land of the Munchkins		1 in the west
b ☐ The land of the Winkies		2 in the south
c ☐ The land of the Quadlings		3 in the east

6 **MP3** **Listen again and tick (✓) T (true), F (false) or D (doesn't say).**

	T	F	D
a Dorothy meets three Munchkins.	☐	☐	☐
b The Winkies have to work for the witch who rules their land.	☐	☐	☐
c Glinda takes Dorothy back to Kansas.	☐	☐	☐

e-ZONE ONLINE ACTIVITIES Before Reading

1 THE CYCLONE

It's always hot and windy on the prairies• in Kansas. The hot sun and the strong wind make everything grey. They make the grass grey. They make the flowers grey. They make the houses grey. They even make people's faces grey.

Dorothy lives in the middle of a big prairie in Kansas. She lives with her Uncle Henry and Aunt Em. Uncle Henry has got a small farm there. Their house is made of wood and it has only got one room. There isn't much furniture in it. There's an old stove• for cooking and a cupboard for the cups and plates. There's a table and three or four chairs and two beds. Uncle Henry and Aunt Em's big bed is in one corner. Dorothy's little bed is in another corner.

There isn't an attic• and there isn't a real cellar•. There's only a small, dark hole under the floor. The family go there when there's a cyclone•. They call the hole 'the cyclone cellar'. Cyclones are very strong winds and they're very dangerous. They move quickly and break everything in their path•. There are often cyclones in Kansas.

GLOSSARY

- **attic:** room in a house under the roof
- **cellar:** room in a house under the floor
- **cyclone:** violent storm with the air moving very fast in a circular direction
- **path:** way; road; track
- **prairies:** large areas of flat grassy land in North America
- **stove:** piece of equipment for cooking or heating

Uncle Henry and Aunt Em work very hard. They work from morning to night. Uncle Henry looks after the cows, the horses and the chickens. Aunt Em looks after their small house. They never smile or laugh. There isn't much happiness in their lives. Poor Uncle Henry and Aunt Em!

Dorothy lives with them because she's an orphan. She hasn't got a mother or father. Her best friend is her little dog. His name is Toto. He has got long, black hair, black eyes and a little nose. Dorothy loves him very much. Toto plays all day and Dorothy plays with him. He's very funny and he makes her happy.

BEST FRIENDS

Who is your best friend?
What do you do with your best friend?

Uncle Henry is sitting outside the door of his small house. He's worried. He's looking at the sky. It's full of black clouds. There's a very strong wind, too. It's blowing• across the prairies. It's making a loud whistling noise•.

Suddenly Uncle Henry stands up.

'A cyclone is coming!' he shouts. 'Dorothy! Em! Go into the cellar! Quick!'

GLOSSARY

- **blowing:** moving air
- **whistling noise:** high sound that a strong wind makes

Aunt Em runs out of the house. She sees the black cone in the sky. She's afraid because the cone is moving fast towards their house.

'Dorothy!' Aunt Em shouts. 'Come here! We must go in to the cyclone cellar!' She opens the little door in the floor and starts to climb down into the hole.

Dorothy picks up Toto and runs into the house. Poor Toto! He's afraid too. He jumps out of Dorothy's arms and runs under the bed. Dorothy runs after him and pulls him out.

'Dorothy!' Uncle Henry calls. 'Quick! Come into the cellar! The cyclone is coming!'

Dorothy starts to run to the little door in the floor but the cyclone hits the house before she can get there. Everything in the room is shaking. The cups and the plates fall on the floor. Dorothy falls on the floor too. BUMP! She can't stand up again.

GLOSSARY

- **climb down:** move by going down
- **cone:** (here) see illustrations on pages 15 and 16
- **picks up:** lifts with her hands
- **shaking:** making little quick movements

Then the wind picks up the house and carries it away. The little house spins• slowly round and round in the cone of the cyclone. Up and up it goes. Soon it is high in the sky. Dorothy and Toto are very frightened. Toto starts barking•.

'It's alright, Toto,' Dorothy says to him. 'I'm here.'

The wind carries the house for miles and miles. Now Dorothy can stand up because the house isn't spinning any more. She goes and sits on her bed. She holds Toto in her arms and waits. Hours pass. It gets dark outside. The wind continues to blow. Toto falls asleep. Dorothy isn't afraid any more. She closes her eyes and falls asleep too.

- **barking:** the noise that a dog makes
- **spins:** turns round and round

2 THE LAND OF THE MUNCHKINS

BUMP! Suddenly the house hits the ground. Dorothy wakes up.

'Good morning, Toto,' she says. Toto wakes up too and puts his cold little nose in her face.

The house isn't moving now. Dorothy looks around and listens. It's light now and the room is full of sunshine! She can hear birds.

'Where are we, Toto?' she says. 'We aren't in Kansas. There aren't any birds there.'

The little dog jumps off the bed and goes to the door. He starts barking. Dorothy follows him. She opens the door and looks out.

'Oh!' she says. 'Oh, what a wonderful place!'

She can see a beautiful country in front of her. There's green grass everywhere. There are tall trees with all kinds of fruit on them. There are brightly coloured birds in the branches of the trees. There are lots of flowers and pretty butterflies. There's a stream of clear water.

It's very different from the grey prairies of Kansas.

GLOSSARY

- **butterflies:** 
- **hits the ground:** falls down to earth
- **stream:** very small river

Then Dorothy sees some people. They are coming towards the house. There are three men and one woman. They are very strange. They are small but they are old. The men have got long beards and the woman has got white hair and lots of wrinkles. They're all wearing tall hats. There are bells on them. The bells make a tinkling noise when the people move their heads. The men's hats are blue and their clothes are blue too. The woman's hat is white. Her dress is also white and it's covered with silver stars. She walks up to Dorothy and says:

'Welcome to the land of the Munchkins! Thank you for killing the Wicked Witch of the East for us. Now our people are free.'

CLOTHES

Look at the picture on page 18.
What's Dorothy wearing?
What are you wearing today?
Tell a partner.

'You're very kind but you're wrong,' Dorothy replies. 'I don't know the Wicked Witch of the East.'

'Look!' the old woman says. 'She's there! Under your house! You can see her feet!'

GLOSSARY

- **beards:** 
- **bells:** 
- **silver:** shiny grey/white colour like metal
- **tinkling:** high sound of small bells
- **wicked:** very bad
- **witch:** woman with magic powers
- **wrinkles:** lines on a person's face when they are old

Dorothy looks and sees a pair of feet in silver shoes. She can't see the rest of the body because it's under the house.

'Oh dear! What can we do?' Dorothy cries.

'Nothing,' the woman says. 'The witch is dead and the Munchkins are happy.'

'Who are the Munchkins?' Dorothy asks.

'They live in this land,' the woman replies.

'Are you a Munchkin?'

'No, I'm not. But I'm their friend. I'm the Witch of the North.'

'Are you a real witch?' Dorothy asks. 'Aunt Em says that witches are bad.'

'There are bad witches and good witches,' the woman says. 'I'm a good witch.'

'Are there many witches here?' Dorothy wants to know.

'There are four witches in Oz,' the Witch replies. 'Well, only three now because the Wicked Witch of the East is dead.'

'And are you all good witches?'

'No, we aren't. The Witch of the South is a good witch. She lives in the land of the Quadlings. But the Witch of the West is very, very wicked.'

Then she picks up the silver shoes and gives them to Dorothy.

'These shoes are for you,' she says. 'You must wear them. They're very special.'

THE SILVER SHOES

Why do you think the shoes are special?
What can the shoes do?
What kind of activities do you need special shoes for?

The shoes are very pretty. Dorothy takes them and puts them on. They are her size and fit• her perfectly.

'Thank you,' she says. 'It's very nice here but I want to go back to Kansas. Can you tell me the way?'

The Munchkins and the Witch look at Dorothy, and they shake• their heads.

'There's a big desert around the land of Oz. Nobody can cross it,' the Witch says.

Dorothy starts crying. The Munchkins start crying too. The Witch takes off• her hat and puts it on her nose.

'One, two, three!' she says. The hat changes into a blackboard. There are some words on it.

'Is your name Dorothy?' she asks.

'Yes, it is,' the girl replies.

'I have a message for you.'

The Witch reads the words on the blackboard:

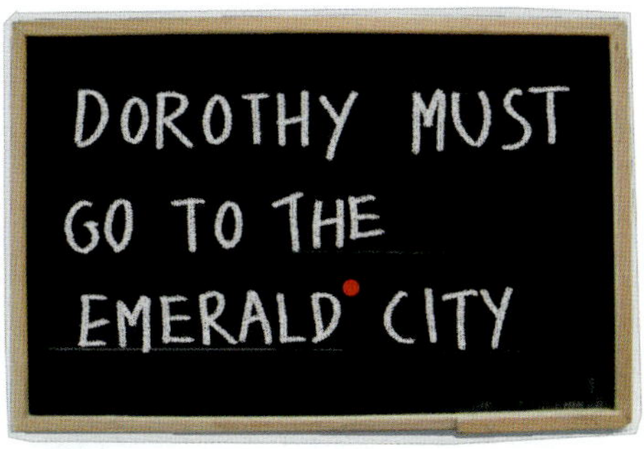

'Where's the Emerald City?' Dorothy asks.

'It's in the middle of Oz,' the Witch replies. 'The Great Wizard of Oz lives there. You must ask him to help you.'

'Is it far?'

'Yes, it's a long way and you must walk there.'

GLOSSARY

- **emerald:** precious green stone
- **fit:** are the right size
- **shake:** move from left to right to say 'no'
- **takes off:** removes

The Witch kisses Dorothy on her head. Her kiss leaves a silver mark•.

'Nothing can hurt you now,' she says. 'Follow the yellow brick• road.'

Then she disappears in the air.

'We must go too, Dorothy,' the Munchkins say. 'Goodbye!' And they walk away into the trees.

Dorothy goes into her house, takes her basket and fills it with bread. Then she washes her hands and face and puts on a clean dress. Now she's ready to meet the Great Wizard of Oz.

'Come on, Toto!' she says. 'Let's go and look for the yellow brick road!'

GLOSSARY

- **brick:** a small block used for building walls
- **mark:** sign

3 THE SCARECROW•

Dorothy finds the road easily and she and Toto start their long journey to the Emerald City. She doesn't feel sad any more. It's a sunny day and the birds are singing. There are pretty blue fences• along the road. There are fields of yellow corn•. She can see the small, round houses of the Munchkins everywhere. They're blue too.

Dorothy and Toto walk for a long time along the yellow brick road. They don't meet anyone. Dorothy is very tired.

'Let's stop and rest for a few minutes, Toto,' she says. 'It's a long way to the Emerald City.'

They sit down on the grass next to a field of yellow corn. There's a scarecrow on a pole• in the middle of it. Its head and body are full of straw•. It's wearing an old blue hat, old blue clothes and a pair of old blue boots. Dorothy looks at it for a long time. The Scarecrow looks at her. Then it winks• at her slowly.

Dorothy's very surprised. She stands up and walks across the field to it.

- **corn:** yellow plant used to produce flour
- **fences:** 
- **pole:** long thin stick of wood or metal
- **scarecrow:** see picture on page 30
- **straw:** dried yellow stems of corn or other cereal
- **winks:** quickly closes and opens one eye

'Good afternoon!' the Scarecrow says with a big smile.

'Oh! Can you speak?' Dorothy says.

'Of course,' he replies. 'Can you take me off this pole, please? It isn't very comfortable. I can't move.'

Dorothy takes the Scarecrow off the pole and puts him on the ground. He's very happy. He moves his arms and legs and shakes his head. Straw flies everywhere.

'Thank you very much,' he says. 'I feel wonderful now.'

'How strange!' Dorothy thinks. 'This man made of straw can speak and move like a real person.' But she doesn't say anything.

'What's your name?' the Scarecrow asks. 'And where are you going?'

'My name's Dorothy,' the girl says, 'and I'm going to the Emerald City. I want to speak to the Great Oz. I want to ask him to send me back to Kansas.'

'Where's the Emerald City?' he asks. 'Who's Oz?'

'Don't you know him?' Dorothy says.

'No, I don't. I don't know anything,' he replies sadly. 'I haven't got a brain•. There's only straw in my head.'

'Oh,' Dorothy says. 'I'm sorry. He's a wizard.'

'Can the Great Oz give me a brain?'

'I don't know,' Dorothy says. 'Come with me to the Emerald City and ask him.'

GLOSSARY

- **brain:** the part of our head that controls movement, thought, memory and feeling

'That's very kind of you. Thank you,' the Scarecrow says.

Toto looks at him and starts barking.

'It's alright,' Dorothy says. 'He doesn't bite•.'

'I'm not afraid of him,' the Scarecrow says. 'I'm made of straw. I'm only afraid of one thing.'

'What's that?' Dorothy asks.

'Fire!'

FEAR

Why is the Scarecrow afraid of fire?

What are you afraid of?

They start walking along the yellow brick road. The Scarecrow tells Dorothy his story and time passes quickly. They walk many miles before they stop to rest again. Dorothy and Toto are hungry.

'Let's have something to eat!' Dorothy says. She sits down on the grass and takes the bread out of her basket. She offers a piece to the Scarecrow.

'No, thank you,' he says. 'I'm never hungry. Tell me about Kansas!'

Dorothy describes the prairies to him.

'Why do you want to go back there?' he asks. 'It's beautiful here. I think Kansas is a sad place to live.'

GLOSSARY

- **bite:** use teeth to cut or hurt
- **sighs:** breathes out slowly making a soft sound

'You haven't got a brain so you don't understand,' Dorothy says. 'My Uncle Henry and Aunt Em are there. I love them. And there's no place like home.'

The Scarecrow sighs•.

'Come on! It's time to go!' she says. 'It's still a long way to the Emerald City.'

The Scarecrow picks up her basket and they start walking again.

e·ZONE ONLINE ACTIVITIES Chapters 1-3

4 THE TIN WOODMAN AND THE LION

In the evening they see a little cottage in the trees. They decide to go in. There are a lot of dead leaves in one corner. Dorothy's very tired. She lies down on the leaves with Toto and they fall asleep immediately. The Scarecrow stands near the door. He's never tired and he never sleeps.

HUNGRY AND TIRED

Why is the Scarecrow never hungry and never tired?

The next morning they leave the cottage and look for a stream of fresh water. Dorothy wants to wash her hands and face. Then she and Toto eat some bread for breakfast. Now she's ready to start walking again. Suddenly they hear a noise in the trees. Someone is groaning.

'Who is it?' Dorothy asks. She's a bit afraid.

'Let's go and see,' the Scarecrow says.

She follows him into the forest. A man made of tin is standing next to a big tree. He's holding an axe in his hands. He isn't moving at all but he's groaning.

GLOSSARY

- **axe:** 
- **cottage:** small house
- **groaning:** making a long low sound
- **tin:** a soft silver-white metal, used in the past for pots and pans
- **woodman:** person working in the woods and cutting trees down

'Can we help you?' Dorothy says.

'Yes!' the man says. 'There's an oilcan in the cottage. Bring it here and put some oil on my arms and legs, please.'

Dorothy runs back to the little house. She finds the oilcan and goes back to the Tin Woodman. First she puts some oil on his neck. Then she puts some on his arms and finally she puts some on his legs.

'That's much better! Thank you very much!' the Tin Woodman says. He turns his head and bends his arms and legs. 'When it rains, I get wet and then I can't move. Water is very bad for my body.' Toto barks at him but the Tin Woodman isn't afraid of him.

'Who are you?' he asks. 'And what are you doing here?'

'I'm Dorothy and this is the Scarecrow,' Dorothy explains. 'We're going to see the Great Oz in the Emerald City. I want to ask him to send me back to Kansas. The Scarecrow wants to ask him for a brain.'

'I haven't got a heart,' the Tin Woodman says. 'Can Oz give me one?'

'I don't know,' Dorothy replies. 'Come with us and ask him.'

'Thank you,' the Tin Woodman says. He picks up his oilcan and they all start walking back to the yellow brick road.

The road takes them into a dark forest. There isn't much light because the sunshine can't get through the branches of the trees. There aren't many birds now. They like sunny fields, not dark forests. The only noises are strange noises. Animal noises!

GLOSSARY

- **bends:** moves arms at the elbows and legs at the knees
- **get wet:** become covered in water
- **heart:** the part of our chest where we feel emotions
- **oilcan:** a metal container for putting oil onto machine parts
- **sunshine:** the light and heat of the sun
- **wild animals:** animals not looked after by people, e.g. lions

Dorothy wonders what kind of animals are making the noises. Toto knows. Dangerous wild animals•! He stays very near to Dorothy and he's very quiet.

WILD ANIMALS

Sort the letters and find the names of some of the animals in the forest.

a) noil _______ b) areb _______

c) griet _______ d) owlf _______

Suddenly a big lion jumps out of the trees. It roars loudly. It hits the Scarecrow and the Tin Woodman with its paws and they fall over. Toto runs up to it and barks. The Lion opens its mouth and shows its teeth. Dorothy forgets to be afraid. She can only think about Toto. She goes up to the Lion and hits it on the nose with her basket.

'Don't bite my dog!' she cries angrily. 'He's very small and you're big.'

The Lion rubs his nose with his paw.

'You're a coward!' she says.

'I know,' the Lion replies sadly and starts crying. 'I make a lot of noise but I'm not brave like other lions. I haven't got any courage.'

Now Dorothy feels sorry for him.

'We're going to the Emerald City to see the Great Oz,' she says. 'I want to ask him to send me back to Kansas. The Scarecrow wants to ask him for a brain and the Tin Woodman wants to ask him for a heart. Come with us! You can ask him for some courage.'

The Cowardly Lion smiles.

'Thank you,' he says.

The four travellers set off down the road to the Emerald City. The Lion walks next to Dorothy. Toto is still a bit afraid of him but they are soon good friends.

GLOSSARY

- **courage:** ability to control fear
- **coward:** someone who isn't brave
- **fall over:** fall to the ground
- **paws:** feet of an animal
- **roars:** the noise that a lion makes
- **rubs:** moves hands (or paws) firmly over something
- **set off:** begin their journey

WOOF!

5 THE JOURNEY

When night comes, they stop under a big tree. The Tin Woodman cuts some wood and makes a fire for Dorothy. She and Toto eat some bread and the Lion goes into the forest to find something for his dinner. The Scarecrow collects• some nuts• for Dorothy's breakfast. Then the little girl and her dog lie down and sleep until morning.

The next day they set off again very early. They walk a few miles and then they come to a big ditch•. It's very wide and very deep. There are a lot of sharp rocks at the bottom of it.

'How can we cross the ditch?' Dorothy asks her friends.

'We can't fly over it,' the Scarecrow says. 'And we can't jump over it. So we must stay here.'

The Lion looks at the ditch and says, 'I can jump over it.'

'Can you?' the Scarecrow says. 'That's good! You can take us across on your back, one by one.'

'Who wants to go first?' the Lion says. He's a bit afraid but he wants to help his friends.

'Me!' the Scarecrow says and he gets on the Lion's back. The Lion jumps across the ditch easily. Then he jumps back and takes Dorothy and Toto. Finally he takes the Tin Woodman across the ditch.

The Lion is tired after his five big jumps•.

'Let's rest before we start walking again,' he says.

GLOSSARY

- **collects:** (here) finds
- **ditch:** a long hole usually around a field to collect water
- **jumps:** when you push yourself off the ground with your legs and feet
- **nuts:** dry fruit with hard shells
- **raft:** a flat boat made of pieces of wood (see illustration)

Later in the afternoon they come to a wide river. They can see a beautiful country on the other side of it. There are green fields and a lot of flowers. They can also see the yellow brick road.

'How can we cross the river?' Dorothy asks.

THE RIVER

How can Dorothy and her friends cross the river?

Make a list of ways with a partner.

'Easy!' the Scarecrow replies. 'The Tin Woodman can cut down some trees and build a raft•. We can cross the river on that.'

'You haven't got a brain,' the Lion says, 'but you have got some good ideas, Scarecrow!'

The Tin Woodman takes his axe and cuts down some small trees. Then he starts to make a raft. The Scarecrow and Dorothy look for some nuts and fruit for dinner. The Lion and Toto sleep in the sunshine. It's late when the Tin Woodman finishes the raft.

'We can't cross the river now,' he says. 'It's dark. We must wait until tomorrow.'

Dorothy, Toto and the Lion make their beds under the trees. When she falls asleep, Dorothy dreams about Kansas.

The next morning they all get on the raft. The Tin Woodman and the Scarecrow have very long poles. They push their poles into the mud• at the bottom of the river and the raft moves. But the water is flowing• very fast. It takes them down the river and far from the yellow brick road on the other side. The Tin Woodman and the Scarecrow can't touch the bottom with their poles any more.

'This is very bad,' the Tin Woodman says. 'We're going towards the land of the Wicked Witch of the West.'

'We must go back and find the yellow brick road,' the Scarecrow says. He pushes his pole very hard into the mud but it gets stuck•. He can't pull it out again! The raft moves away and he's still holding his pole in the middle of the river.

'Goodbye!' he shouts to the others.

They look at him sadly. They don't want to leave him there.

GLOSSARY

- **flowing:** moving continuously
- **gets stuck:** can't move
- **mud:** soft wet earth

'We must rescue• him,' the Lion says. 'I have an idea! Hold my tail•, Woodman!'

The Tin Woodman takes his tail and the Lion jumps in the water and starts swimming. Slowly, slowly, he pulls the raft to the side of the river.

Just then a stork• flies over the river. She sees them and stops.

'Who are you and where are you going?' she asks.

'I am Dorothy,' the girl answers, 'and these are my friends, the Tin Woodman and the Cowardly Lion. We're going to the Emerald City.'

'This isn't the right road,' the Stork says.

'I know,' Dorothy says, 'But we have another friend, the Scarecrow. He's in danger and we don't know how to help him.'

'Where is he?' the Stork asks.

'He's over there. He's on a pole in the middle of the river. We can't go without him. We must rescue him.'

'I can help you,' the Stork says. 'I can bring him to you.'

'You're very kind,' Dorothy says. 'He's made of straw so he isn't heavy.'

The big bird flies into the air and over the water. She picks up the Scarecrow and takes him to the side of the river.

The Scarecrow is very happy to be with his friends again and they are happy to see him.

'Thank you, Stork!' he says.

'That's all right. I'm happy to help but I must go now. I must look after my children,' the kind Stork replies and flies away.

- **rescue:** save from danger
- **stork**: see bird in illustration
- **tail:** the part that sticks out at the back of an animal

Dorothy, the Scarecrow, the Tin Woodman and the Lion set off along the river. Toto sometimes runs in front of them and sometimes behind them.

Suddenly they enter a meadow• of big scarlet• poppies. Their scent• is so powerful that Dorothy feels quite sleepy. She keeps walking until she can stand no longer and falls down in the meadow.

'What shall we do?' the Tin Woodman asks.

'If we leave her here she will die,' the Lion says. 'The smell of the flowers is killing us all. I can't keep my eyes open, and the dog is asleep already.'

'Run fast,' the Scarecrow says to the Lion, 'and get out of this deadly• flowerbed• as soon as you can. We will bring the little girl with us.'

The Lion runs as fast as he can but he falls asleep before he is out of the poppy field.

The Scarecrow and the Tin Woodman are not affected• by the scent of the flowers. They make a chair with their hands and carry Toto and Dorothy to a pretty place beside the river. Then they go back for the Lion. The Tin Woodman builds a truck and, with the help of a large number of field mice•, they pull the Lion out of the poppies into the green fields.

The sweet fresh air revives• Dorothy, Toto and the Lion. Soon they find the yellow brick road and continue their journey to the Emerald City.

GLOSSARY

- **affected:** when something causes a change
- **deadly:** dangerous because it can cause death
- **field mice:** type of mice living in fields
- **flowerbed:** area where flowers are planted
- **meadow:** field with grass and wild flowers
- **revives:** wakes up and makes strong again
- **scarlet:** red
- **scent:** smell; perfume

6 THE EMERALD CITY

The four travellers see a beautiful green light in the sky in front of them.

'That's the Emerald City,' Dorothy says. 'Come on! It isn't far now!'

Soon they come to a big green wall. There's a gate in it. It's glittering in the afternoon sun. Dorothy looks at it carefully. It's made of emeralds! There's a bell next to the gate so she rings it. The gate opens and they all go inside. A little man in green clothes is standing there with a big box.

'What do you want in the Emerald City?' he says.

'We want to see the Great Oz,' Dorothy replies.

'It's important,' the Scarecrow says.

'I am the Guardian of the Gate,' the little man in green says. 'I can take you to his Palace. But before you go there, you must put on these glasses.'

He takes five pairs of glasses out of the box. The glass in the glasses is emerald green.

'Why?' Dorothy asks.

'Everyone in the Emerald City wears them,' the Guardian of the Gate says.

GLOSSARY

- **gate:** door in the city walls
- **glass:** transparent substance for making windows, bottles, glasses
- **glasses:** 
- **glittering:** shining with short quick flashes of light

GREEN GLASSES

Why do you think everyone in the Emerald City wears green glasses?

They put on the glasses. Even Toto has a pair. Then the guardian takes a big gold key and opens another gate. Dorothy is amazed. Everything is green – the houses, the streets and the pavements•. Even the sky is green. Children are buying green lemonade with green money. Men in green clothes are pushing green carts• along the green streets. Everybody is smiling.

The Guardian of the Gate takes them through the streets to a big building in the middle of the city. A soldier with a green moustache• and a green uniform is standing in front of the door.

'These people want to speak to the Great Oz,' he says to the soldier. 'Please tell him they are here.'

The soldier goes away. When he comes back he says, 'Oz can see you but not today. You must stay in the Palace for a few days.'

A young girl takes them to their rooms. They are beautiful and very comfortable. Dorothy sleeps very well that night.

- **carts:** vehicles with two or four wheels pulled by horses
- **moustache:**

- **pavements:** paths with hard surfaces for walking on

After breakfast the next day the young girl comes back to Dorothy's room. She's carrying a green silk• dress and a green silk apron•. She asks Dorothy to put them on and she takes her to the Throne• Room.

'You must go in alone,' she says.

Dorothy opens the door and walks in. The room is big and round and it has an arched• roof. The walls, the floor and the ceiling are made of emeralds. They glitter in the light. The throne is in the middle of the room and it's made of emeralds, too. Dorothy looks at it in surprise. There's an enormous head on it! Suddenly the mouth on the head opens and starts to speak.

'I am Oz. Who are you and what do you want?' it says.

Dorothy is a bit afraid but she replies:

'I am Dorothy. I want your help. I want to go back to Kansas.'

Oz's eyes look up, then down, then left, then right.

'I can help you but you must help me.'

'What must I do?' Dorothy asks.

'Go to the land of the Winkies and kill the Wicked Witch of the West!'

'Oh, no!' Dorothy cries. 'I don't want to kill anybody.'

'You must,' Oz says. 'You have the silver shoes and the silver mark from the Good Witch of the North. Nothing can hurt you.'

Dorothy goes back to her room. She's very sad. She lies on her bed and cries.

GLOSSARY

- **apron:** something you wear to keep the front of your clothes clean
- **arched:** 
- **silk:** thin smooth soft cloth
- **throne:** special chair for a king or queen

The next morning a soldier with a big green moustache takes the Scarecrow to see Oz.

The Scarecrow opens the door and he sees a beautiful woman with wings. She looks at him and says in a sweet voice:

'I am Oz. Who are you and what do you want?'

'I am the Scarecrow. My head is full of straw. I'd like a brain. Can you give me one?'

'Yes, I can. But first you must help me.'

'What must I do?' the Scarecrow asks.

'Go to the land of the Winkies and kill the Wicked Witch of the West!' she says.

The next morning the soldier with the green moustache takes the Tin Woodman to see Oz.

The Tin Woodman opens the door and he sees an ugly monster. It has five eyes, five arms and five legs. It looks at him and roars:

'I am Oz. Who are you and what do you want?'

'I am the Tin Woodman. I'm made of tin and I haven't got a heart. Can you give me one?'

'Yes, I can. But first you must help me.'

'What must I do?' the Tin Woodman asks.

'Go to the land of the Winkies and kill the Wicked Witch of the West!'

The next morning it's the Lion's turn to speak to Oz.

THE LION'S QUESTION

What does the Lion want?

The Lion opens the door and he sees a big ball of fire. He's afraid. A voice from the ball of fire says:

'I am Oz. Who are you and what do you want?'

'I am the Cowardly Lion. I'm afraid of everything. Can you give me some courage?'

'Yes, but you must help me.'

'What must I do?' the Lion asks.

'Go to the land of the Winkies and kill the Wicked Witch of the West!'

The Lion leaves the Throne Room and goes to find his friends.

'What can we do?' Dorothy asks sadly.

'We must go to the land of the Winkies and kill the Wicked Witch,' the Lion says.

7 THE WICKED WITCH

The next day the soldier with the green moustache takes them to the Guardian of the Gate. They give him back their glasses and he opens the gate.

'Which road goes to the land of the Winkies?' Dorothy asks.

'There isn't a road because nobody goes there,' he replies.

'How can we find the Wicked Witch?' Dorothy asks.

'You must walk to the west, where the sun goes down,' he says. 'She's a very bad witch. Be careful!'

They thank him and start walking across the fields towards the west. The grass is soft under their feet and there are flowers everywhere. Dorothy is still wearing the silk dress and apron but they aren't green now. They're white.

They walk for a long time. The land changes. It isn't flat any more. There are a lot of hills. The grass isn't soft now and there aren't any flowers or trees. That evening Dorothy, Toto and the Lion sleep on the hard grass under the stars.

The Wicked Witch of the West is watching them from her castle. She has only got one eye but she can see very far with it. She is angry.

'What do they want?' she says. 'Why are they in my country?'

She takes out a silver whistle• and blows it once. Wolves come from all directions to her castle. They have long legs and sharp• teeth.

'Find the strangers• and kill them,' she says.

The Tin Woodman and the Scarecrow aren't asleep. They hear the wolves. The Scarecrow starts shaking but the Woodman isn't afraid.

'This is my fight, my friend,' he says to the Scarecrow. 'Stand behind me!'

The Tin Woodman holds his axe above his head. When the wolves arrive, he cuts off their heads one by one.

In the morning Dorothy sees the bodies of the wolves. She's frightened but the Tin Woodman explains everything. She thanks him for saving them and, after breakfast, they start walking again.

GLOSSARY

- **sharp:** thin and pointed
- **strangers:** people you don't know
- **whistle:** something that you put in your mouth and blow to make a high sound

The Wicked Witch is very angry about the wolves. She takes her silver whistle again and blows it twice. This time big crows• fly to her castle from all directions. They have sharp beaks•.

'Find the strangers and kill them!' she says.

Dorothy and her friends look up and see the birds in the sky.

'This is my fight,' the Scarecrow says. 'Lie down on the ground! Everyone!'

FIGHTING THE CROWS

Why does the Scarecrow say 'This is my fight'?

The Scarecrow opens his arms wide. When the crows come, the Scarecrow breaks their necks one by one.

'It's safe now,' he says to his friends. 'We can continue our journey.'

GLOSSARY

- **beaks:** hard pointed part of a bird's mouth
- **crows:** large black birds with a rough cry

The Witch is very, very angry. She takes her silver whistle again and blows it three times. Thousands of black bees arrive at the castle.

'Find the strangers and kill them!' she says.

Dorothy sees the bees and cries:

'What can we do?'

'Take out my straw!' the Scarecrow says to the Tin Woodman. 'Cover Dorothy, Toto and the Lion with it!'

When the bees arrive, they find only the Tin Woodman. They try to sting• him but they can't hurt his tin body. Soon all the bees are dead because a bee can't live after it stings.

The Witch is furious. There's only one way she can destroy these strangers. She must ask the Winged Monkeys to help her. She goes to her cupboard and takes out a Golden Cap. She puts it on her head and says some magic words.

Immediately the sky goes dark. There's a noise of wings and of laughing and chattering•. The Winged Monkeys are coming! They fly into the castle and stop in front of the Witch. They all have big strong wings on their shoulders.

• **chattering:** making short high noises, like monkeys

• **sting:** make a small hole in the skin so that you feel a sharp pain

'What can we do for you?' the King of the Monkeys asks her.

'Find the strangers in my land,' the Witch says. 'Kill the people and the dog but don't kill the Lion. Bring him to me! He's strong. He can work for me.'

The Monkeys fly away immediately. When they find Dorothy and her friends, they pick up the Tin Woodman. They take him to a place where there are a lot of sharp rocks and drop him. Poor Woodman! His tin body breaks on the rocks. He can't move.

Next they catch the Scarecrow. They pull all the straw out of his hat and clothes and throw them into the top of a tall tree. Then they put a rope around the Lion's neck and take him back to the Witch's castle.

Dorothy watches. She's holding Toto in her arms. She's very frightened. The King of the Monkeys flies up to her. He's holding his long hairy• arms out in front of him and he has a horrible smile on his face. Then suddenly he stops. His smile disappears. He picks Dorothy and Toto up carefully and takes them back to the castle.

A CHANGE OF PLAN

Why doesn't the King of the Monkeys kill Dorothy?

The Witch is waiting for them. She's surprised to see Dorothy.

'Why is she here?' she asks the King of the Monkeys.

'This girl has the mark of the Good Witch of the North on her head,' he replies. 'We can't hurt her.' Then he and the other Monkeys fly away.

The Witch looks at Dorothy and sees the silver shoes on her feet. She knows they are special shoes. She wants them. But how can she take them from the girl? She must wait for the right moment. She takes her to the kitchen.

'You are my slave• now!' she says. 'You must work for me.'

'You must wash the floor every day!' she says. 'Then you must do the washing-up! And don't forget! I'm watching you!'

GLOSSARY

- **hairy:** with lots of hair
- **rope:** strong thick string

- **slave:** person who must work without receiving money

8 THE RESCUE

8 The days pass. Dorothy works very hard in the kitchen. She remembers Uncle Henry and Aunt Em in Kansas. She remembers her friends the Scarecrow and the Tin Woodman. She's very sad and she often cries. At night she goes to see the Lion. The Witch doesn't give him anything to eat or drink so Dorothy takes him food and water from the kitchen. Then she lies down next to him, puts her head on his warm body and sleeps until the morning.

The Witch watches Dorothy all the time. She's waiting for the right moment to take the silver shoes. Dorothy wears them all the time. She loves them. The only time she takes them off is when she has a bath. The Witch doesn't like water so she's afraid to go near the girl when she's in the bath.

One day Dorothy is cleaning the kitchen and she slips• on the wet floor. She falls over and one of the silver shoes comes off. The Witch is watching. She picks it up quickly and puts it on.

'Give me back my shoe!' Dorothy says.

'No! It's my shoe now,' the Witch replies.

'You're a wicked woman!' Dorothy shouts. 'I want my shoe!'

GLOSSARY

• **slips:** falls over on water or ice

There's a bucket• of water near the door. The girl picks it up and throws the water over the Witch.

'Aarrgh!' the Witch cries. 'Water is the end of me!' And she starts to disappear in front of Dorothy's eyes.

'I'm going,' she says. 'Going, going, going.'

In another minute there's just a big brown puddle• of water on the kitchen floor. Dorothy quickly takes her shoe, puts it on again and runs outside.

'The Witch is dead!' she shouts. The Winkies look at her in surprise. They are also the Witch's slaves.

'We're all free now!' she says to them.

They start cheering• and shouting.

'The Wicked Witch is dead! We're free! Thank you, Dorothy!'

Dorothy goes to the Lion and takes the rope off his neck.

- **bucket:** metal or plastic container for carrying things in, for example water
- **cheering:** shouting because they are happy
- **puddle:** small pool of water

He's very happy to be free again. But then he remembers their friends, the Scarecrow and the Tin Woodman and he becomes sad.

'Can we find them, Dorothy?' he asks.

'We can try,' Dorothy replies. 'Let's ask the Winkies to help us!'

The Winkies are very happy to help. They go immediately and rescue the broken body of the Tin Woodman and bring it back to the castle.

'Can you make him better?' Dorothy asks.

'Yes, we can,' they say. They work day and night for three days. On the fourth day the Tin Woodman and the Lion walk into Dorothy's room.

'Thank you for saving me, Dorothy!' the Tin Woodman says.

'Now we must rescue the Scarecrow,' Dorothy says to the Winkies. 'Can you help us again?'

THE SCARECROW

Where are the Scarecrow's clothes?

Dorothy, the Lion and the Tin Woodman take the Winkies to the tall tree. The Winkies can't climb the tree so the Tin Woodman cuts it down with his axe. Then they take the Scarecrow's clothes, boots and hat back to the castle. They fill them with clean straw and the Scarecrow is a new man!

'Thank you for saving me, Dorothy!' the Scarecrow says.

The friends stay with the Winkies in the castle for a few days. Then Dorothy says:

'We must go back to the Great Oz and tell him that the Witch is dead.'

'Yes,' the Tin Woodman says. 'I want my heart.'

'And I want my brain,' the Scarecrow says.

'And I want some courage,' the Lion says.

'And I want to go back to Kansas,' Dorothy says. 'Let's leave tomorrow!'

Before they go, Dorothy goes to the Witch's cupboard.
She fills her basket with food for the long journey. She sees the Golden Cap. It's very pretty so she puts it on.

Then they say goodbye to the Winkies. The Tin Woodman cries because he's sad to leave them. He likes the Winkies very much and they like him.

The friends start walking. There isn't a road to follow and soon they are lost in a big field of tall grass. They meet the Queen of the Mice there.

'Excuse me!' Dorothy says to her. 'We're lost. Can you tell us the way to the Emerald City?'

'It's very far,' the Queen replies. Then she sees the Golden Cap on Dorothy's head. 'Why don't you use the magic of the cap and ask the Winged Monkeys to take you there?'

'How can I do that?' Dorothy asks.

'Look inside the cap! The magic words are there,' she says and disappears in the long grass.

Dorothy looks inside the cap and says the magic words and the Winged Monkeys immediately fly down from the sky.

'What can we do for you?' the King says.

Dorothy feels a bit afraid of him. She remembers their last meeting. But she says in a loud clear voice:

'We want to go to the Emerald City. Can you take us there?'

'Of course!' the King replies.

The monkeys pick the friends up and fly across the sky with them in their arms. The journey is long but the monkeys fly fast. Soon Dorothy can see the glittering green gate of the Emerald City below them.

9 THE WIZARD OF OZ

The four travellers ring the bell on the Gate. The Guardian is surprised to see them.

'You're back from the Land of the Winkies!' he says.

'Yes, we are,' Dorothy says. 'We want to see the Great Wizard!'

The Guardian takes them to the Palace of Oz. They eat a good dinner and go to bed early.

There's no message from the Wizard the next day. Or the next. Or the next. The Scarecrow is angry.

'Tell the Wizard we want to see him tomorrow!' he says to the soldier with the green moustache. 'Tell him we have the Golden Cap and we can call the Winged Monkeys.'

The soldier comes back with a message from the Wizard.

'Go to the Throne Room at nine o'clock tomorrow morning!' he says.

The next morning they meet outside the Throne Room. The soldier with the green moustache takes them in. There isn't anyone there. There's only a big screen• in a corner.

Suddenly a voice says:

'I am Oz. Who are you and what do you want?'

'It's me, Dorothy,' the little girl says. 'I'm here with my friends the Scarecrow, the Tin Woodman and the Lion. Do you remember your promises to us? The Witch of the West is dead so you must send me back to Kansas.'

GLOSSARY

- **screen:** a large flat panel that can be moved around to make a smaller area in a room

'And give me a brain,' the Scarecrow says.

'And give me a heart,' the Tin Woodman says.

'And give me some courage,' the Cowardly Lion says.

'I must think about it,' the voice says. 'Go away and come again tomorrow.'

'No!' the Tin Woodman says. 'We can't wait any longer.'

The Lion roars loudly. Toto is frightened and jumps. His tail hits the screen and it falls over. The four friends turn their heads to look. To their surprise, they see a little old man in the corner. He is very surprised, too.

'Who are you?' the Tin Woodman says. He lifts his axe in the air.

'I am Oz, the Great Wizard,' the little old man says. 'Please don't hurt me!'

'But the Wizard is a big head!' Dorothy says.

'No, he's a beautiful woman with wings,' the Scarecrow says.

'No, he's a monster with five eyes, five arms and five legs,' the Tin Woodman says.

'He isn't. He's a ball of fire,' the Lion says.

'You are all wrong,' the man says. 'They are only tricks.'

'If you aren't the Great Wizard, who are you?' Dorothy asks.

'The people here believe that I'm the Great Wizard but I'm just a man from Omaha.'

'Omaha! That isn't very far from Kansas!' Dorothy says.

'No, it isn't, but it's very far from here,' the man replies.

The Tin Woodman asks him about his promises.

'I'm sorry,' the man says. 'I can't keep my promises to you.'

'Then you're a very bad man!' Dorothy says.

'No, my dear! I'm a very good man but I'm a very bad Wizard.'

'But what about my brain?' the Scarecrow says.

'And my heart?' the Tin Woodman says.

'And my courage?' the Cowardly Lion says.

'Very well,' he says. 'Come back tomorrow.'

'Can you send me back to Kansas?' Dorothy asks.

'Give me three days to think about it,' the little man says. 'Stay in my palace and enjoy yourselves. But, please! Don't tell anyone in the Emerald City about my tricks. They must be a secret between you and me.'

e-ZONE ONLINE ACTIVITIES Chapters 7-9

GLOSSARY

- **Omaha:** the largest city in the state of Nebraska in the USA
- **tricks:** things that are not really what they seem to be, e.g. magic tricks

10 THE HOT-AIR BALLOON

The next morning the Scarecrow goes to see Oz.

'Have you got my brain?' he asks.

'Yes, I have. Sit in this chair, please. I must take off your head,' Oz says.

Oz takes off the Scarecrow's head and goes into a small room. He takes out the old straw and puts in a lot of new straw. Then he goes back and puts the new head on the Scarecrow.

'How do you feel now?' Oz asks.

'I feel very intelligent,' the Scarecrow says. 'Thank you very much.'

Then it's the Tin Woodman's turn.

'Have you got my heart?'

'Yes, I have. Sit in this chair, please,' Oz says. 'I must make a hole in your body.'

He makes the hole and puts a beautiful silk heart inside the Tin Woodman's body.

'Oh, thank you!' the Tin Woodman says. 'I feel wonderful. I'm very happy to have a heart.'

Finally the Lion goes to see Oz.

'Have you got some courage for me?' he asks.

'Yes, I have,' Oz says.

He takes a square green bottle off a shelf. There's some liquid in it. He puts the liquid in a dish and gives it to the Lion.

'Drink this!' he says.

'What is it?' the Lion asks.

'Courage!' Oz says.

The Lion drinks the liquid.

'How do you feel now?' Oz asks.

'I feel very, very brave!' the Lion says happily.

'Now, how can I send Dorothy back to Kansas?'

Oz thinks for three days. On the fourth day, Dorothy goes to the Throne Room.

'We must make a hot-air balloon,' Oz says.

'A hot-air balloon! Why?' the girl asks.

'Kansas is on the other side of the big desert. We can fly across it in a balloon!'

'Are you going back home, too?' Dorothy asks.

'Yes,' Oz says. 'I'm tired of my life in the Emerald City. I want to go back to Omaha.'

Dorothy helps Oz to make the balloon. They use green silk, ropes and a big basket. They work for three days. It's a very big balloon. Then they fill it with hot air. The ropes hold it to the ground so it can't fly away.

Then Oz sends a message to all the people in the Emerald City.

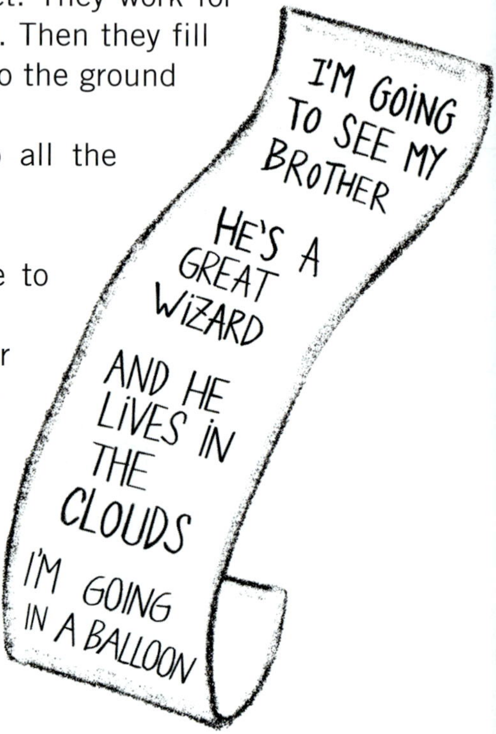

Everyone comes to the Palace to see it. Oz gets in the basket first.

'Now the Scarecrow is your ruler•,' he says to the people in a loud voice. 'You must do what he says.'

The big balloon is pulling the ropes. They're breaking.

'Dorothy!' Oz calls. 'Get in! Quick!'

Dorothy picks up Toto and runs to the balloon. She's very near it when, CRACK! the ropes break and the balloon goes up into the sky without her.

'Come back!' she shouts. 'I want to go, too!'

'I can't,' Oz shouts. 'Goodbye!'

Dorothy starts crying. What can she do now? How can she cross the desert?

GLOSSARY

- **ruler:** a person who controls a country

The Scarecrow has an idea.

'Let's ask the soldier with the green moustache!' he says.

He calls the soldier.

'Dorothy wants to cross the desert,' the Scarecrow says to him. 'What must she do?'

'She must go and see Glinda, the Witch of the South,' the soldier says. 'She rules the land of the Quadlings. Her castle is very near the desert.'

'Glinda's a good witch, isn't she?' Dorothy asks.

'The Quadlings think she is good,' the soldier replies. 'She's kind to everyone. She's also young and very beautiful.'

'How can I get to her castle?' Dorothy asks.

'You must go south,' he says. 'But the road is dangerous for travellers.'

'Thank you,' Dorothy says and the soldier leaves them.

'We must go and ask Glinda for help,' the Scarecrow says.

'We?' Dorothy says. 'Are you coming too?'

'Of course!' the Scarecrow, the Tin Woodman and the Lion say together.

'I'd like to leave tomorrow morning,' Dorothy says.

'Let's go and get ready for the journey then!' the Scarecrow says.

The next day they get up early and set off for the land of the Quadlings.

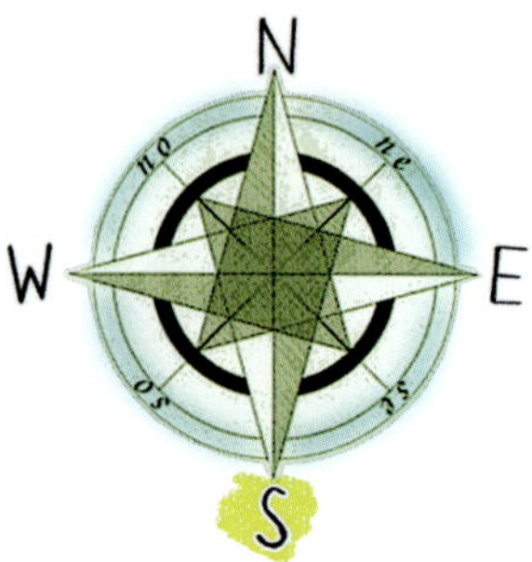

11 THE LAND OF THE SOUTH

They cross green fields full of flowers and butterflies. The Lion is very happy to be out of the city and in the country again. Toto is, too.

On the second day of their journey they come to a forest. It's very big and very dark. They're a little afraid but they know that they must go through it. The Scarecrow goes first. He finds a space between two big trees.

'Come on!' he says. 'We can go in here.'

Suddenly a big branch of one of the trees bends• down, picks him up and throws him on the ground. He finds another space and tries again. The same thing happens. A branch bends down, picks him up and throws him on the ground.

'That's strange,' Dorothy says. 'What can we do?'

'Let me try!' the Tin Woodman says.

He goes up to the first tree. When the branch bends down to pick him up, he cuts it off with his axe. The tree starts shaking. The Tin Woodman quickly runs under its branches and goes into the forest.

'Follow me!' he shouts. 'These trees are the policemen of the forest. It's their job to keep people out.'

The other trees don't hurt them and the friends walk through the forest without any problems.

GLOSSARY

- **bends:** makes a curve

When they come out of it, they see a high wall in front of them. It's made of white china•.

'We must climb over it,' the Scarecrow says. 'But we haven't got a ladder•!'

'I can make one,' the Woodman says. He goes and looks for some wood in the forest. Dorothy, Toto and the Lion are tired. They lie down on the grass and sleep.

The ladder is ready when they wake up. One by one they climb it. Soon they are all sitting on top of the china wall. They look at the country in front of them.

It's flat and white, like a plate. There are many small houses made of china. They're half the size of Dorothy. They're painted in bright colours.

There are also pretty little farms with china fences around them. There are many cows and sheep and horses and pigs and chickens, all made of china. Even the people are made of china.

GLOSSARY

- **china:** material used for making cups, plates, etc.
- **ladder:** 

The friends jump off the wall and start walking. They walk very carefully because the people are very small and they don't want to break them.

Then Dorothy sees a princess. She's beautiful and she's wearing a very pretty dress. When she sees the strangers, she runs away.

'Stop!' Dorothy says. 'I want to talk to you. You are very beautiful. Can I put you in my basket and take you back to Kansas with me?'

'Oh, no!' the Princess says. 'I'm very happy here. I can run and play and talk. In Kansas I must stand on a shelf in a sitting room all day. I don't want to do that.'

'Yes, of course,' Dorothy says. 'I understand. Well, goodbye, Princess!'

They continue walking and soon they get to the other side of the china country. The wall isn't very high here and they can climb over it easily.

Now they are in the forest again. They can hear the noises of wild animals. Toto is afraid. Dorothy's afraid too, but they continue walking. Soon they arrive in an open space. There are hundreds of animals there – tigers, elephants, bears, wolves, foxes – all kinds of animals.

'They're having a meeting,' the Lion says.

He goes up to them. The animals stop talking and look at him.

'Welcome, King of the Forest!' the animals say.

'Why are you having a meeting? What's your problem?' the Lion asks.

The animals tell him about a monster in the forest.

'It's enormous. It has eight legs. It creeps through the forest and catches animals. Then it eats them!' a tiger says.

'Where is this monster now?' the Lion asks.

'In those trees,' the tiger says.

The Lion walks slowly towards the trees. The monster is asleep. It's an enormous spider. It's very ugly. It has a big body and a big head but its neck is very thin. The Lion jumps on its back. CRACK! He breaks its thin neck with his paw. The spider's head falls on the ground.

The Lion goes back to the forest animals and tells them that the monster is dead. They are very happy.

'Please stay and be our king,' they say.

'I can't stay now because I'm taking Dorothy to the Land of the Quadlings,' he says. 'But I promise to come back.'

12 THE GOOD WITCH

12 When the friends come out of the dark forest, they see a very big hill in front of them. There are big rocks all over it.

'What can we do?' Dorothy says. 'We can't climb that hill!'

'Call the Winged Monkeys, Dorothy!' the Woodman says. 'They can help us. They can fly over the hill.'

Dorothy puts on the Golden Cap and says the magic words. The Monkeys arrive immediately.

'Can you take us to the land of the Quadlings?' Dorothy asks.

'Yes, of course,' the King replies.

The monkeys take the friends over the hill and put them down in the land of the Quadlings.

Dorothy looks around. It's a beautiful country. The fences and houses are bright red and the corn in the fields is bright yellow. The people are short and fat and their clothes are red. They all have happy smiles on their faces.

They stop at a farm and ask the farmer's wife the way to Glinda's castle. It isn't far and soon they are standing outside the castle gate. There are three pretty girls in red dresses in front of it. One of them takes Dorothy and her friends to a room inside the castle. Dorothy washes her hands and face and combs her hair. Then the girl in the red uniform comes back and takes them to Glinda.

The Witch of the South is sitting on a throne made of rubies•. She's very beautiful. She has long red hair and blue eyes and she's wearing a white dress. She smiles at Dorothy.

'What can I do for you?' she says.

'I want to go back to Uncle Henry and Aunt Em in Kansas,' Dorothy says.

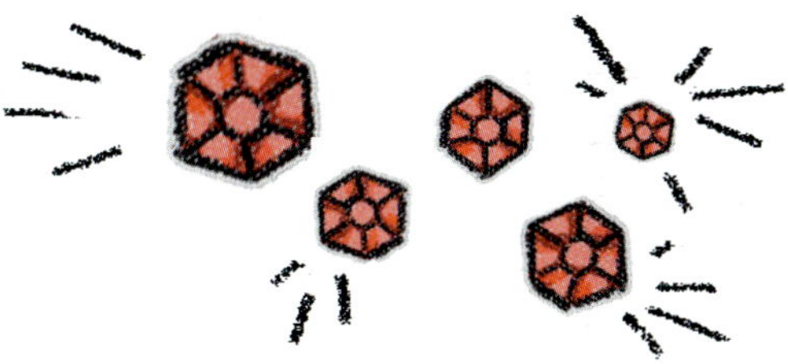

GLOSSARY

• **rubies:** precious red stones

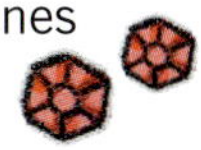

Glinda bends down and kisses her.

'I can send you back to Kansas,' she says. 'But you must give me the Golden Cap.'

Dorothy takes off the cap and gives it to Glinda.

'What about your friends?' the Witch says. 'What do they want to do?' She looks at the Scarecrow.

'I want to go back to the Emerald City,' he says. 'The people there like me and I want to be their ruler.'

'I like the Winkies and they like me,' the Tin Woodman says. 'The Wicked Witch of the West is dead now and they're free. I'd like to be their ruler.'

'I don't want to live in a city. The forest is my home,' the Lion says. 'I'd like to be king of all the animals in the forest.'

Glinda puts on the Golden Cap and calls the Winged Monkeys.

'Take the Scarecrow back to the Emerald City. Then take the Tin Woodman to the land of the Winkies. After that take the Lion to the forest!' she says to the King.

'But what about me?' Dorothy asks. 'How can I get back to Kansas? The Winged Monkeys can't take me there.'

'Your silver shoes can take you there, Dorothy,' the Witch says. 'Knock• your heels together three times and tell them where you want to go. That's all!'

It's time for the friends to say goodbye. Dorothy kisses the Scarecrow, the Tin Woodman and the Lion.

GLOSSARY

- **knock:** hit

'Goodbye,' she says.

'Goodbye, Dorothy. And thank you,' they say. The Tin Woodman is crying. Dorothy starts crying too. She's sad to leave her new friends. Glinda comes down from her throne and kisses Dorothy goodbye.

'Thank you for your help,' Dorothy says to her.

Then she picks up Toto, closes her eyes, knocks her heels together three times and says:

'Take me home to Uncle Henry and Aunt Em in Kansas!'

A strong wind takes her up into the sky. She can hear and feel the wind but she can't see anything. BUMP! Now she's sitting on the grass outside her small house on the Kansas prairie. Toto jumps out of her arms and runs away. Dorothy looks at her feet. She isn't wearing the silver shoes any more.

She stands up and looks around. There's Aunt Em in the garden! And there's Uncle Henry in the field! She starts running towards them.

'Aunt Em! Uncle Henry!' she cries. 'It's me, Dorothy! I'm home!'

e·zone ONLINE ACTIVITIES Chapters 10-12

AFTER READING TALK ABOUT THE STORY

1 Read each question and circle the number that is most true for you.

1 = No, not at all. **5** = Yes, absolutely

a I enjoyed reading the story.
1 2 3 4 5

b The story is easy to understand.
1 2 3 4 5

c I think the story is for people of my age.
1 2 3 4 5

d I'd like to see the film. OR I'd like to see the film again.
1 2 3 4 5

e Dorothy is different from the children in traditional fairy tales.
1 2 3 4 5

2 There are descriptions of several parts of the Land of Oz in the story. Write a short description of a part of your country.

AFTER READING COMPREHENSION

1 Are the following sentences true (T) or false (F)? Tick (✓).

		T	F
a	Uncle Henry and Aunt Em haven't got much free time.	☐	☐
b	The Munchkins grow corn.	☐	☐
c	The Scarecrow knows the Wizard of Oz.	☐	☐
d	Dorothy is angry with the Lion because he tries to bite Toto.	☐	☐
e	The Scarecrow falls into the river.	☐	☐
f	The Wizard knows that Dorothy's silver shoes are special.	☐	☐
g	The Winkies are the slaves of the Wicked Witch of the East.	☐	☐
h	The Winkies rescue the Scarecrow's clothes from the top of a tall tree.	☐	☐
i	The Wizard of Oz isn't a real wizard.	☐	☐
j	Oz wants to help the four friends.	☐	☐
k	The China Princess wants to go to Kansas with Dorothy.	☐	☐
l	Glinda uses the Golden Cap to send Dorothy back to Kansas.	☐	☐

2 **Match the two halves of the sentences.**

a ☐ Dorothy doesn't want to stay in the Land of Oz
b ☐ The Witch of the North gives Dorothy the silver shoes
c ☐ The Scarecrow gets stuck in the river
d ☐ The Wizard tells Dorothy that nothing can hurt her
e ☐ The Winkies have to work for the Wicked Witch
f ☐ Dorothy calls the Winged Monkeys
g ☐ The balloon leaves without Dorothy
h ☐ Dorothy isn't wearing the silver shoes when she arrives back in Kansas

1 because the ropes break.
2 because he pushes his pole deep into the mud.
3 because she doesn't need them any more.
4 because she needs their help to get back to the Emerald City.
5 because she knows they can help her.
6 because they are her slaves.
7 because she has the silver shoes and the silver mark on her head.
8 because it isn't her home.

AFTER READING CHARACTERS

1 Write the name of a character, or characters, in the spaces.

a .... is Dorothy's best friend.
b .... is killed by Dorothy's house.
c .... jumps across a ditch five times.
d .... builds a raft.
e .... has a Golden Cap in her cupboard.
f .... mend the Tin Woodman.
g .... must do what the person with the Golden Cap says.
h .... becomes the new ruler of Oz.

2 Match the colours to the characters.

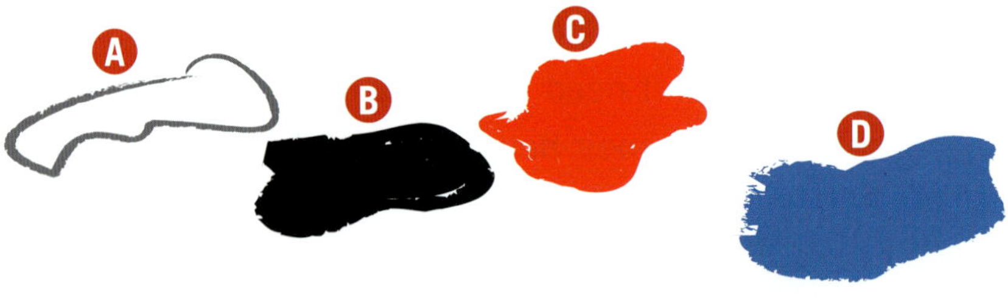

1 ☐ Toto
2 ☐ the Munchkins
3 ☐ the Quadlings
4 ☐ the Witch of the North
5 ☐ the Guardian of the Gate

3 What colour do you think the Winkies' clothes are?

4 Who says the following? Match the characters to the sentences.

a ☐ 'I can help you but you must help me.'
b ☐ 'Find the strangers and kill them.'
c ☐ 'This is my fight, my friend! Stand behind me!'
d ☐ 'In Kansas I must stand on a shelf in a sitting room all day.'
e ☐ 'What can I do for you?'

1 The China Princess
2 The Wizard of Oz
3 Glinda
4 The Wicked Witch of the West
5 The Tin Woodman

5 In pairs answer the questions below.

a How does Dorothy help the Scarecrow?
b How does she help the Tin Woodman?
c How does the Lion help his friends?
d How do the Scarecrow and the Tin Woodman help each other in the land of the Winkes?
e How does the Wizard of Oz help the four friends?
f Is the Wizard a good person or a bad person? Explain your answer.

NEW

AFTER READING VOCABULARY

1 Match the words in the box with their meaning.

stove	throne	failure	stream	
scent	corn	rope	ruler	paws

a the opposite of success ....

b feet of an animal ....

c thing you use for cooking or heating ....

d very small river ....

e yellow plant used to produce flour ....

f smell; perfume ....

g special chair for a king or queen ....

h strong thick string ....

i person who controls a country ....

2 Complete the sentences with the correct form of the verbs in the box.

carry	cross	fly	go	lie	reply	say	try

a 'You're a coward,' Dorothy .... – 'I know,' the Lion .... sadly.

b The Monkeys .... into the castle and stop in front of the Witch.

c The Lion .... all the friends on his back and they .... the river.

d In the book, Dorothy .... to find a way to go back home.

e The little girl .... down and sleeps until morning.

f 'Come on, Toto! Let's .... and look for the yellow brick road!'

3 Complete the sentences with words in the box.

wizard	tricks	whistle	monkeys
land	slave	ladder	size

a The Wizard can do .... but not true magic.

b 'Which road goes to the .... of the Winkies?'

c The people in the Land of the South are half the .... of Dorothy.

d The old man is a good man but a bad ....

e The .... help those who wear the Golden Cap.

f 'You are my .... now!' the Witch says. 'You must work for me!'

g 'We must climb this wall, but we haven't got a ....!'

h The Witch blows a silver .... and the wolves come immediately.

4 Read the sentences below. Is *'s* a verb (V) or a possessive (P)? Tick (✓).

		V	P
a	It*'s* wearing an old blue hat.	☐	☐
b	The woman*'s* gloves are white.	☐	☐
c	The Scarecrow collects some nuts for Dorothy*'s* breakfast.	☐	☐
d	Dorothy*'s* an orphan.	☐	☐
e	The Monkeys put a rope around the Lion*'s* neck.	☐	☐
f	The Winkies are also the Witch*'s* slaves.	☐	☐

AFTER READING LANGUAGE

1 Read the extract from the story. Complete it with the words below.

across at into out of outside towards up

Uncle Henry is sitting **(a)** .... the door of his small house. He's worried. He's looking **(b)** .... the sky. It's full of black clouds. There's a very strong wind too. It's blowing **(c)** .... the prairies. It's making a loud whistling noise.

Suddenly Uncle Henry stands **(d)** ....

'A cyclone is coming!' he shouts. 'Dorothy! Em!

Go **(e)** .... the cellar! Quick!'

Aunt Em runs **(f)** .... the house. She sees the black cone in the sky. She's afraid because the cone is moving fast **(g)** .... their house.

2 Put a sign (▲) where the word in brackets goes in each sentence.

a Dorothy is an orphan she lives with her aunt and uncle. (so)

b The Land of Oz is nice Dorothy wants to go home to Kansas. (but)

c The Scarecrow isn't heavy he's made of straw. (because)

d It's late the Tin Woodman finishes the raft. (when)

e The Winged Monkeys drop the Tin Woodman in a place there are a lot of sharp rocks. (where)

3 **Make adjectives from the verbs using *–ed* or *–d* . Then use the adjectives to complete the sentences.**

bore	frighten	tire	surprise	interest

- **a** Dorothy is .... when she sees the Wizard behind the screen.
- **b** Toto is .... when the Lion roars.
- **c** Dorothy is .... after walking all day.
- **d** Oz is .... with his life in the Emerald City.
- **e** The Scarecrow isn't .... in food.

4 **Choose adjectives from the box and complete the sentences.**

boring	frightening	interesting	surprising	tiring

- **a** The wild animals in the forest are ....
- **b** Life on the prairies is .... because there's nothing to do.
- **c** Cleaning the Wicked Witch's castle is very .... work.
- **d** It's not .... that Dorothy wants to go home.
- **e** Oz is a strange but .... place.

5 **K** **Work with a partner. Tell him/her about:**

- **a** a school subject you think is boring.
- **b** a school subject you are interested in.

AFTER READING PLOT AND THEME

1 What happens in the story? Put the events a–j on the timeline in the correct order.

1	2	3	4	5	6	7	8	9	10
i									

a They go to the land of the Winkies.

b The Wizard of Oz leaves Oz in a balloon.

c The Witch of the North gives Dorothy special silver shoes.

d Dorothy kills the Wicked Witch and she and her friends go back to see the Wizard.

e Dorothy and her friends go to see the Witch of the South.

f The Wizard of Oz tells the four friends to kill the Wicked Witch of the West.

g Dorothy discovers that the silver shoes can take her back to her home in Kansas.

h The Wicked Witch tries to kill them.

i A strong wind carries Dorothy and her dog Toto to the Land of Oz.

j Dorothy makes friends with a scarecrow, a tin woodman and a lion.

2 **One theme of the story is 'home'. What is Dorothy's home like? Tick (✓) true (T) or false (F).**

		T	F
a	The land around the farm is very flat.	☐	☐
b	The farmhouse is big and comfortable.	☐	☐
c	Dorothy has her own bedroom.	☐	☐
d	Her uncle and aunt work hard.	☐	☐
e	Her uncle and aunt are always happy.	☐	☐
f	Dorothy has lots of friends in Kansas.	☐	☐

3 **In pairs answer the questions.**

a What do you think Dorothy likes about her home?
b What do you like best about your home?

4 **Another theme of the story is knowing the things we already have. Dorothy, the Scarecrow, the Tin Woodman and the Lion all want things they already have. Find examples in the story of this. Then tell the class.**

5 **What are your good points? How do you use them? Write some sentences about yourself.**

I'm tall so I'm good at playing basketball.

....

....

....

....

....

NEW

AFTER READING CAMBRIDGE ENGLISH EXAMS

K Cambridge English: Key English Test Reading and Writing Part 2

1 Think of the story. Choose the best word (A, B or C) for each space.

1 '.......... we help you?' Dorothy says.
A can't **B** must **C** can

2 'When it rains, I get wet and then I .... move.'
A mustn't **B** can't **C** must

3 'How .... we cross the ditch? ' Dorothy asks her friends.
A mustn't **B** can **C** can't

4 '.......... you tell us the way to the Emerald City?'
A can't **B** can **C** must

5 'Oh no!' Dorothy cries. 'I don't want to kill anybody' 'You .... ', Oz says.
A must **B** can **C** can't

6 Oz: 'I .... help you but you .... help me' 'What .... I do?'
A can't **B** can **C** must
A must **B** can't **C** can
A can **B** must **C** can't

7 'I'd like a brain. .... you give me one?'
A mustn't **B** must **C** can

8 'You .... go to the land of the Winkies and kill the Wicked Witch.'
A must **B** can **C** mustn't

9 'You .... put on these glasses.'
A can **B** must **C** can't

10 'The girl has the grey mark of the Good Witch and we .... hurt her!"
A can **B** mustn't **C** must

K Cambridge English: Key English Test Reading and Writing Part 5

2 Read the short summary of the book. Choose the best word (A, B, or C) for each space.

The Wonderful Wizard of Oz is **(1)** .... modern fairy tale. A little girl called Dorothy lives **(2)** .... the dry, grey prairies of Kansas. **(3)** .... life is boring and her dog Toto is her only friend. But after a cyclone carries away her house, her life becomes full **(4)** .... surprising adventures. She makes new friends and together they meet many strange people. The places they visit are wonderful. **(5)** .... are castles, talking animals, witches and dark forests. But **(6)** .... the end Dorothy **(7)** .... that there's **(8)** .... place like home!

1	**A** some	**B** a	**C** no
2	**A** on	**B** to	**C** at
3	**A** their	**B** since	**C** her
4	**A** A of	**B** on	**C** by
5	**A** A they	**B** there	**C** here
6	**A** A on	**B** from	**C** in
7	**A** A goes	**B** learns	**C** looks
8	**A** A some	**B** no	**C** a

K Cambridge English: Key English Test Reading and Writing Part 7

3 Complete the description. Write ONE word in each space.

My name is Oz and I **(1)** .... in a wonderful land. People say that I am a **(2)** .... wizard. But I am only **(3)** .... good man and not a great wizard. The characters in this story think that I can give them all that they **(4)** .... me for. So I help them to understand that they already **(5)** .... what they ask for. In the room where I live, the walls, the floor and the ceiling are made **(6)** .... emeralds. My throne is in the middle of the room. I can look like an enormous head, like a beautiful woman, like **(7)** .... ugly monster or like a big ball of fire. But these are only **(8)** .... It is not real magic. Like Dorothy, I want to go home, too. We **(9)** .... a big balloon and fly home. I like it here, but I think that there's no **(10)** .... like home!

AFTER READING EXIT TEST

1 MP3 **Listen and tick (✓) the correct picture.**

1 a

b

2 a

b

3 a

b

4 a

b

2 Circle the correct answer.

a Where's Aunt Em when the cyclone arrives?
1 in the fields **2** outside the door **3** inside the house

b What is the last thing that the Witch of the North gives Dorothy?
1 directions **2** a kiss **3** silver shoes

c Who does the Lion take across the ditch first?
1 the Scarecrow **2** Dorothy **3** The Tin Woodman

d What is there in the Guardian of the Gate's box?
1 a key **2** hats **3** glasses

e What does the Scarecrow see when he goes to see the Wizard?
1 a big head **2** a woman **3** a monster

f What happens when the Wicked Witch blows her silver whistle twice?
1 wolves come **2** crows come **3** bees come

g What must Dorothy do to use the magic of the Golden Cap?
1 say some magic words
2 call the Winged Monkeys
3 knock her heels together

h What kind of heart does the Wizard give the Tin Woodman?
1 a silk one **2** a paper one **3** a tin one

i What does the Lion kill in the forest?
1 another lion **2** a tiger **3** a spider

j What colour is Glinda's dress?
1 red **2** blue **3** white

e-ZONE ONLINE ACTIVITIES After Reading

AFTER READING PROJECT

1 **WEB Follow the links on the website and find out more about the man who did the original illustrations for *The Wonderful Wizard of Oz*.**

a Look at the illustrations for *The Wonderful Wizard of Oz*.
Do you prefer the Dorothy in the original version or the Dorothy in this book?

b Read about William Wallace Denslow.
In which American city did L. Frank Baum and W. W. Denslow meet?

c Draw the characters from the story. How do you imagine the Emerald City?